D1636030

HAWKEYE COLLINS & AMY ADAMS in

THE MYSTERY OF THE
STAR SHIP
MOVIE & 8 OTHER MYSTERIES

by M. MASTERS

Spotlight reinforced library bound edition copyright © 2007. Spotlight is a division of ABDO Publishing Company, Edina, Minnesota.

All stories written by Alexander von Wacker
Illustrations by Brett Gadbois
Editor: Kathe Grooms
Assistant Editor: Louise Delagran
Design: Terry Dugan
Production: John Ware, Donna Ahrens
Cover Art: Robert Sauber

ISBN-10 1-59961-144-9 (reinforced library bound edition)
ISBN-13 978-1-59961-144-0 (reinforced library bound edition)

Library of Congress Cataloging-In-Publication Data
This title was previously cataloged with the following information:

Masters, M.
    Hawkeye Collins & Amy Adams in The mystery of the Star ship movie & 8 other mysteries.
    (Can you solve the mystery?™ ; #7)
    Summary: Two twelve-year-old sleuths, "Hawkeye" Collins and Amy Adams, solve nine mysteries using Hawkeye's sketches of important clues.
    [1. Mystery and detective stories. 2. Literary recreations.] I. Title. II. Title: Hawkeye Collins and Amy Adams in The mystery of the star ship movie & 8 other mysteries. III. Title: Mystery of the Star ship movie & 8 other mysteries. IV. Series: Masters, M. Can you solve the mystery? ; #7.
PZ7.M42392Hf   1983   [Fic]   83-17318

CONTENTS

READ THE SOLUTIONS IN YOUR MIRROR

Amy Adams

Hawkeye Collins

Young Sleuths Detect Fun in Mysteries

By Alice Cory
Staff Writer

Lakewood Hills has two new super sleuths watching over its citizens. They are Christopher "Hawkeye" Collins and Amy Amanda Adams, both 12 years old and sixth-grade students at Lakewood Hills Elementary.

Christopher Collins, the popular, blond, blue-eyed sleuth of 128 Crestview Drive, is better known by his nickname, "Hawkeye." His father, Peter Collins, who is an attorney downtown, explains, "We started calling him Hawkeye many years ago because he notices everything, even tiny details. That's what makes him so good at solving mysteries." His mother, Linda Collins, a real estate agent, agrees: "Yes, but he

Sleuths continued on page 4A

Sleuths continued from page 2A

also started to draw at a very early age. His sketches capture everything he sees. He draws clues or the scene of the crime — or anything else that will help solve a mystery."

Amy Adams, a spitfire with red hair and sparkling green eyes, lives right across the street, at 131 Crestview Drive. Known to many as the star of the track team, she is also a star math student. "She's quick of mind, quick of foot and quick of temper," says her teacher, Ted Bronson, chuckling. "And she's never intimidated." Not only do she and Hawkeye share the same birthday, but also the same love of mysteries.

"If something's wrong," says Amy, leaning on her ten-speed, "you just can't look the other way."

"Right," says Hawkeye, pulling his ever-present sketch pad and pencil from his back pocket. "And if we can't solve a case right away, I'll do a drawing of the scene of the crime. When we study my sketch, we can usually figure out what happened."

When the two detectives are not playing video games or soccer (Hawkeye is the captain of the sixth-grade team), they can often be seen biking around town, making sure justice is done. Occa-

sionally aided by Hawkeye's frisky golden retriever, Nosey, and Amy's six-year-old sister, Lucy, they've solved every case they've handled to date.

How did the two get started in the detective business?

It all started last year at Lakewood Hills Elementary's Career Days. There the two met Sergeant Treadwell, one of Lakewood Hills' best-known policemen. Of Hawkeye and Amy, Sergeant Treadwell proudly brags, "They're terrific. Right after we met, one of the teachers had a whole pile of tests stolen. I sure couldn't figure out who had done it, but Hawkeye did one of his sketches and he and Amy had the case solved in five minutes! You can't fool those two."

Sergeant Treadwell adds: "I don't know what Lakewood Hills ever did without Hawkeye and Amy. They've found a dognapped dog, located stolen video games, and cracked many other tough cases. Why, whenever I have a problem I can't solve, I know just where to go — straight to those two super sleuths!"

> **" They've found a dognapped dog, located stolen video games, and cracked many other tough cases. "**

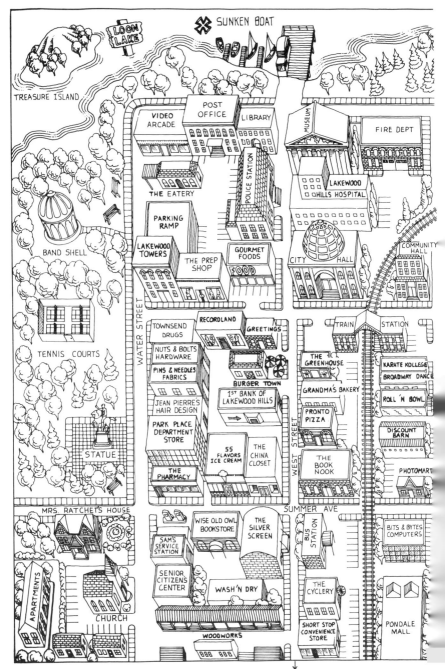

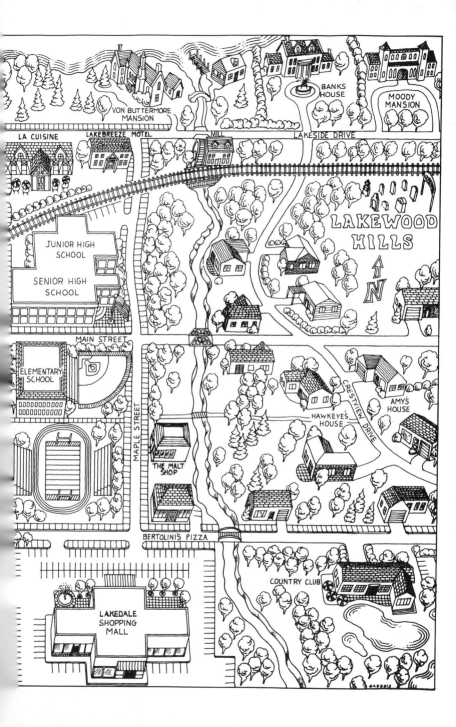

Dear Readers,

You can solve these mysteries along with us! Start by reading very carefully -- Watch out for things like what people <u>say</u> happened, the ways they behave, and details like the time and the weather.

Then look closely at the sketch or other picture clue with the story. If you remember the facts, the picture clue should help you break the case.

If you want to check your answer-- or if a hard case stumps you -- turn to the solutions at the back of the book. They're written in mirror type. Hold them up to a mirror and they'll look right. If you don't have a mirror, turn the page and hold it up to the light. (You can teach yourself to read backwards, too. We can do it prett... well now and it comes in handy som... times in our cases.)

Have fun -- we sure did!

Amy

Hawkeye

The Secret of the Four-Fingered Forger

They were the best pair of sleuths that Lakewood Hills had ever seen. Hawkeye Collins, famous for his sharp eyes and quick hand, could always sketch the scene of a crime and find the hidden clue. Amy Adams, his partner, was the star of the track team, and her mind was as fast as her feet.

Together, the two friends had solved every case they'd had. Just that morning, their observant eyes and quick thinking had averted a potential disaster.

"Good thing you did a drawing of the stage and spotted that crack," said Amy, her red hair blowing as they biked to the bank.

"Yeah, well, I wouldn't have sketched it if you hadn't figured something was wrong," said Hawkeye. "And just think, that whole stage would've collapsed!"

Mrs. von Buttermore, the richest person in town, had bought the old Opera Hall and donated it to the local children's theater. Hawkeye's mother, a real estate agent, thought the hall would be perfect. So did his father, a lawyer who handled all of Mrs. von Buttermore's charitable donations.

"I can't believe that silly old engineer didn't even see the problem." Amy rolled her sparkling green eyes.

"Really! The first big dance number on stage, and the whole show would have gone under—so to speak," replied Hawkeye.

Amy groaned. "Har, har. Hawkeye, I think you'd better stick to solving mysteries."

"Okay, okay."

Hawkeye reached into his back pocket where he always kept his sketch pad. In the same pocket was a twenty-five dollar check. Mrs. von Buttermore had written the check to him and another to Amy for cleaning the Opera House.

"One more check for our savings accounts," said Hawkeye. "That's pretty neat."

They arrived at the First Bank of Lakewood Hills a couple of minutes later. After they leaned their bikes up against the parking meter, they went in and walked up to one of the bank windows. They were all set to deposit their checks, but there were no tellers around.

"This is weird," said Hawkeye.

Amy nodded. "I'll say. Something pretty big must be going on."

With his blond head, Hawkeye nodded toward a group of bank employees gathered to one side of the office.

"It looks like they've got a funny check or something from a drive-in customer," he whispered to Amy.

Amy hurried over to the window by the drive-in lane and returned in a split second.

"There's just a woman in a junky old car out there," she said, flipping a red pigtail over her shoulder. "Doesn't seem too suspicious."

Just then, they overheard two tellers talking excitedly while they stared at the customer at the drive-in window.

"A check for a million dollars from Mrs. von Buttermore!" one of the tellers exclaimed.

"Hey," Hawkeye called to the tellers, "we just came from Mrs. von Buttermore's house and our checks are from her, too."

One of the tellers came over. "They are?" he asked suspiciously as Hawkeye slid his check across the counter.

"Yeah," Amy said eagerly. "We spent a few days cleaning up the old Opera House for her and this is our pay." She showed her check to the teller, too.

The teller examined the checks, then frowned and looked up.

"If you don't mind, I think I'd better have the manager take a look at these," said the teller, pressing a button.

When the manager came over, the teller showed her the checks and explained the situation. Looking concerned, the manager headed toward the rear of the bank. A moment later, she returned with the check for one million dollars. She laid the check on the counter next to Hawkeye's and Amy's checks.

Hawkeye leaned forward and examined the million-dollar check. He noticed something immediately.

"Hey, that's not Mrs. von Buttermore's signature!" he exclaimed. "Look at the way the 't' is crossed."

Amy's eyes opened wide. "Hawkeye, you're right—the signatures are different!"

"That means someone—someone forged Mrs. von Buttermore's signature!" Hawkeye slapped his forehead. He examined the forged check again.

"And look at these four fingerprints up at the top. That't weird. Only three fingerprints and a thumbprint."

Quite alarmed, the teller and the bank manager bent over the checks and studied them.

The manager shook her head. "Uh-oh. I was just about to call Mrs. von Buttermore to verify the million-dollar check. Looks like I should call the police instead!"

As the manager reached for the phone, Amy ran over to the side window and looked out.

"Hey, wait a minute—" she began. "I think the woman's on to us. She's trying to start her car! Wait, she can't start it—she's getting out!"

Hawkeye rushed to the window. "Can you see who it is?" he asked.

"No, I—" Amy squinted. "She's wearing a long coat and a hat. And she's hiding her face."

The manager and the teller scrambled over to the window. The mysterious person looked up, saw them, and tore off in a run.

"After the forger!" cried Amy.

Right behind her, Hawkeye shouted, "We'll catch her!"

The two sleuths dashed out the front doors of the bank. Outside in the bright sunshine, they spotted the forger running out of the bank's drive-in area.

"There!" said Hawkeye.

The woman, her hair stuffed under a hat and her hands concealing her face, turned left onto West Street and ran on.

Amy sped down West Street with Hawkeye just behind her. They chased the forger around the corner and onto Lakeside Drive. Then the woman ducked into a large building.

"She went into the public library!" Amy called to Hawkeye.

Weaving in and out of the crowds of people, Hawkeye and Amy raced down the street. They reached the library and bolted up the steps. Inside, Hawkeye ran up to the information desk.

"Did someone just come running in here?" he asked.

"Why, yes," said the librarian, pointing to a side room. "I didn't see who it was, but I just heard someone run into that reading room."

"Look!" said Amy, pointing to a coat and hat on the floor. "The forger got rid of her stuff!"

Hawkeye and Amy wasted no time. Entering the small reading room, they found five people in it, two men and three women. The door they had come in was the only entrance to the room, though there was an emergency exit in one corner.

"But that door has an alarm," said Amy. "So the forger has got to be one of these people."

Hawkeye reached into his back pocket for his sketch pad and pencil.

"Yeah, we have to figure out which woman is the forger," whispered Amy, walking behind a large bookshelf.

Hawkeye nodded. "Really. She might try to write another bad check."

They made their way behind the bookshelf. Pushing a few books aside, they peered through. The two men stood before the bookshelves on the other side of the room. The three women were seated at a table.

Hawkeye knew that there had to be something in his sketch that would give the forger away.

"I wish we'd been able to see the forger's face," Amy said quietly.

"Yeah, but maybe we'll recognize something else," Hawkeye muttered.

Minutes later, Hawkeye had completed the drawing, and stood staring at it. He knew there had to be something in his sketch that would give the forger away—her clothes, her mannerisms, or perhaps something she carried.

"I know there's a clue in here, Amy," he said, showing her the drawing.

The next moment he had it.

"There it is!" he whispered excitedly.

Amy gasped. "Way to go, Hawkeye!" she whispered back. "You stay here. I'll go call the police—they can take it from here," she added, hurrying off.

WHO FORGED THE MILLION-DOLLAR CHECK?

See page 71

The Case of the Telltale Water

"I'm boiling!" said Hawkeye as he and Amy biked home from school late one afternoon.

"Really!" Amy wiped her forehead. "Every time I leaned on my desk at school today, my arms stuck to it. Boy, am I glad we only have one more week of school."

"And then summer vacation!" said Hawkeye, letting go of his handlebars and waving both hands.

"Catch you later, Amy," Hawkeye said as he coasted into his driveway.

"Does that mean you're going to call me tonight for help with your math?"

"Very funny," Hawkeye snickered.

As Amy steered her bike toward her house, she caught sight of two small bikes sprawled on the front lawn. She shook her head as she parked her ten-speed in the garage. Buffy and Duffy, the terrible twins, were over playing with Lucy, Amy's six-year-old sister.

"I wonder what they're up to now," she thought to herself as she swung open the kitchen door. "There's trouble every time the twins are—"

Amy's left foot skidded in a small puddle of water. She glanced up. "Oh, no!"

Someone had left the kitchen faucet on and the sink was overflowing. A steady stream of water rushed from the sink, down the cabinet, and onto the floor.

"Oh, my gosh!"

Amy threw her books aside and raced over to the sink. A couple of dish towels had plugged the drain.

"Mom!" cried Amy, pushing up her sleeves. "Mom! Dad! Lucy! Mom!"

No one answered.

Amy shut off the faucet and stuck her hand into the icy water. She pulled the dish towels out of the drain and at once the water began to go down.

"Someone's going to be in trouble, and it won't be me," she said, her feet sloshing about in the water. "Drat that Lucy—I'll bet she did it!"

Suddenly Amy heard giggles. She looked through the kitchen window and saw Lucy and the twins goofing around in the back yard. Bernie, Lucy's Saint Bernard, sat panting in the shade.

"Lucy!"

Amy slid the rear door open and hurried into the back yard.

"Lucy, darn you, did you do this?" said Amy, pointing toward the house.

Lucy, who was missing her two front teeth, knew something was wrong. "Huh?"

"What happened?" asked Buffy.

"The sink!" shouted Amy. "Someone left the faucet on and now there's water everywhere."

Lucy, her eyes shifting to either side, glanced at the twins.

"Uh-oh," she said in a hushed voice.

Duffy, the other sandy-haired twin, was quick on the defense. "We've been out here all afternoon playing asteroids."

"Yeah, right," agreed Buffy.

Duffy continued. "See, each of us is a planet. We all spin around. Sometimes we pretend we're a shrinking universe and we come together. Then we burst apart—you know, and make a new universe. Bernie over there is our sun. He's the sun because he's too hot to move and the sun doesn't move, either. We all revolve around him and—"

Amy clenched her fists and shouted, "Lucy, did you leave the faucet on?"

Lucy scratched her head and hesitated for

11

a split second. "No. Maybe it wa*th* Mom. Or Dad. He'*th* not flying today," she said. Their father was an airline pilot.

"Lucy, you know this is Mom's day at the hospital. She won't be home until tonight." Their mother was a doctor. "Where's Dad?"

"He'*th* not here. He left a little while ago." **Lucy glanced at Buffy.** "I think he went shopping."

"Yeah," Buffy said, "he must have left the **faucet on and then gone.**"

From inside the house came the sound of someone slipping on the wet floor. A moment later Hawkeye stepped outside.

"Wow, what happened?" said Hawkeye, math book in hand. "Boy, this place is a mess!"

Amy turned to him. "I came home and the kitchen sink was plugged up. The faucet was on and there was water everywhere!"

Hawkeye nodded toward Lucy and the twins. "Did they have anything to do with it?" he asked, just a bit amused.

Lucy got mad. "We've been out here all afternoon!"

"Right," said Duffy. "We've been out here for a couple of hours at least. We haven't been near the house."

Amy grabbed a handful of her red hair and yanked on it in frustration.

"You're lying," she said to Lucy. "You guys

always get into trouble when you're together."

Hawkeye grinned. "Hey, Amy," he said, "what's the matter with you? Don't you believe your own sister?"

Amy turned to him and rolled her green eyes. "Hardly! Just do a sketch and you'll see why. In fact, do a sketch of this area and let me have it."

Hawkeye sat down on a bench and pulled out a piece of paper from his math book.

"I came over to get help on a math problem. I didn't think you'd have a problem, too," he said, chuckling.

"Hawkeye, it's not funny!" Amy shook her head. "This house is a mess. Now will you just do a sketch and give it to me!"

"Hey, all right! Just be cool," replied Hawkeye.

He quickly drew everything he saw in the area Amy had indicated. Moments later he held up the completed drawing.

"Here you go," he said.

"Thanks!" said Amy, sarcastically.

Drawing in hand, Amy marched over to Lucy.

"Lucy," said Amy, holding the sketch out, "I think you left the faucet on. The proof's right here in Hawkeye's drawing. Now just tell me the truth. Did you leave the water on or didn't you?"

"Lucy," said Amy, "I think you left the faucet on. The proof's right here in Hawkeye,s drawing."

"Ah—ah—" Lucy glanced down at the drawing then back up at Amy.

"She already told you!" shouted Buffy.

Lucy's face flushed red. "Buffy, be quiet! Let me do the talking!" She turned to her big sister. "Well—"

WHY DID AMY THINK THAT LUCY HAD LEFT THE KITCHEN FAUCET ON?

See page 73

The Mystery of the Christmas Caper

"It's Santa Claus!" exclaimed Amy, when the door to the von Buttermore mansion swung open.

Hawkeye looked closely at the man in a Santa suit standing before them.

"Wait a minute," he said, smiling at the man's somewhat uncomfortable expression. "That's Henry."

"Yes, it is I," said Henry, the terribly proper and not very jolly butler. "The annual Christmas party has begun."

He turned and gestured toward the inside of the house. Every corner of the Great Hall was packed with people. Candles, evergreen boughs,

17

and bright Christmas ornaments were everywhere. Two large tables by the wall overflowed with cake, candy, and other Christmas treats.

"Come in at once," Henry continued. "Mrs. von Buttermore is about to receive her gift from the zoo."

"Oh, wow!" exclaimed Hawkeye as he took off his coat. "Look at the size of that tree!"

"Yeah, but look at *that*!" said Amy.

She was pointing to a monkey wearing a red bow around its neck. The monkey was perched on the arm of Mr. Perkins, the zoo director. Just then, Mr. Perkins, who was wearing a festive sprig of holly, stepped into the middle of the room and spoke.

"Quiet, everyone! Quiet!" he announced. "At this time, I would like to present Mrs. von Buttermore with a very special gift—this monkey. His name is Leo. This is our small way of thanking you, Mrs. von Buttermore, for the beautiful new monkey facilities you donated to the zoo. They're the best in the world."

Mrs. von Buttermore, looking elegant in a glittering gown, stepped into the middle of the Great Hall and patted the brown, fuzzy little monkey. "Thank you so much. He's adorable!" she said, smiling.

Mrs. von Buttermore spotted Hawkeye and Amy.

"Oh, I'm so glad you're here," she said. "We

were just about to sing some Christmas carols." She turned to the monkey. "Maybe my little friend here will turn the pages while I play the piano."

As Mrs. von Buttermore held her hand out toward Leo, the monkey's attention was caught by her brilliant Egyptian bracelet. Still sitting on Mr. Perkins's shoulder, the animal reached out.

"He likes your bracelet," said the zoo director, staring at the priceless bracelet himself. "I must admit, it is absolutely stunning."

Mrs. von Buttermore slipped it off her wrist and walked over to the grand piano.

"It is beautiful, isn't it?" she said, setting the piece of jewelry on the piano. "It was part of Grandpapa's collection. But I'm afraid it's a bit too heavy to wear while playing the piano, and now it's time to sing."

She adjusted her shiny gown and sat down at the piano. Everyone applauded, including Leo, who perched himself on a nearby table. Mrs. von Buttermore hummed a few bars, flexed her fingers, and started to play "Jingle Bells." All the people in the huge mansion burst into song.

"Hey, there's Sarge," said Hawkeye, nodding toward the pudgy man at the rear of the room.

It was Sergeant Treadwell, a Lakewood Hills policeman who was one of Hawkeye's and Amy's best friends. They saw him a lot, too, because whenever the sergeant had a case he couldn't solve, he always came to them for help.

The guests grew jollier and merrier as Mrs. von Buttermore played song after song. When she finally stopped, everyone clapped and begged for more.

"Bravo!" shouted Sergeant Treadwell from the rear of the room. "More!"

"Oh, I really couldn't," pleaded Mrs. von Buttermore. "At least, not right now."

She stood and reached for her Egyptian bracelet. It wasn't there.

"Oh, dear!" she gasped. "My bracelet seems to be missing!"

One of the guests exclaimed, "Someone stole Mrs. von Buttermore's priceless bracelet!"

"Now, now," said Mrs. von Buttermore, remaining cool. "Perhaps I just misplaced it."

Hawkeye and Amy ran up to her and looked all around the piano.

"Don't worry, we'll find it, Mrs. von Buttermore," Hawkeye told her.

Mrs. von Buttermore, not sure what to make of the situation, glanced around. "How odd. You don't suppose someone really stole it, do you?"

Sergeant Treadwell raised his hands and shouted, "Everyone remain where you are! The bracelet's got to be in this room and I'm—"

Henry, the butler, broke in. "I say, I did see a gentleman run out that door back there a while ago," he said, pointing to the other end of the Great Hall. "It was the gentleman who brought the monkey."

Hawkeye slapped his forehead. "Mr. Perkins, the zoo director!"

Amy took off. "Come on, Hawkeye!"

The two sleuths cut through the crowd of guests and went out the door Henry had pointed to.

"Which way?" asked Amy.

"Hey, here's a napkin," said Hawkeye, looking down a hall that led to the west wing of the von Buttermore mansion. That part of the house was hardly ever used, and it was dark and deserted.

Hawkeye and Amy started down the long hallway.

"I wonder which room he could be in," Hawkeye said.

"Look," said Amy. "He dropped his sprig of holly by the door to this room. Let's look and see if he's in there."

The large door was ajar, and they slipped through cautiously. They found themselves in the old library.

"He went out the window!" said Amy. "Look, it's open!"

They ran to the window. Outside was a pair of footprints leading through the deep snow and into the cold night.

"You go get Sarge. I'm going to sketch those footprints," said Hawkeye.

Amy began to walk back out of the library. "I'm going to go tell Sarge which way Mr. Perkins went."

"Okay, I'll—" Hawkeye reached into his back pocket and felt nothing. "Hey, where's my sketch pad?" he said.

Then Hawkeye patted the pockets of his sports jacket. "Oh, yeah, I almost forgot." He pulled the sketch pad from the inside pocket of the jacket. "You go get Sarge, Amy. I'm going to sketch those footprints."

"Right." Amy hurried out of the room in search of Sergeant Treadwell.

Hawkeye took a pencil from a nearby table and began sketching. He noticed a shred of torn clothing hanging from the window frame. He drew that, then the notes and books on the desk, and the footprints outside in the snow. He was just putting the final touches on his drawing when Amy returned with Sergeant Treadwell. At that very instant, Hawkeye realized something.

"Hey," he said excitedly, holding up his sketch. "I know what happened to Mrs. von Buttermore's bracelet!"

WHAT HAPPENED TO MRS. VON BUTTERMORE'S BRACELET?

See page 75

The Case of the Double Alibi

In the dark, deep basement of the police station, Sergeant Treadwell put his fingers to his lips, signaling Hawkeye and Amy to be very quiet. They descended a narrow staircase, passed through a long, dimly lit hallway, turned a corner, and came to a blackened room.

"Presto!" exclaimed Sergeant Treadwell, as he flicked on the light switch.

Before them, like gold at the end of a treasure hunt, stood a gleaming ping-pong table.

"Fantastic! It's a beaut," said Hawkeye, grinning.

"I'll say," agreed Amy. "We're going to whomp you, Sarge."

Sergeant Treadwell went over to a cabinet and took out a ball and three new paddles.

"Just be careful," he said. "This is brand new. It's my surprise fiftieth-anniversary present to the station. Besides me, you two are the only ones who know about it."

"Don't worry—my victories are always clean and swift," said Amy, with a grin.

Hawkeye grabbed a paddle. "Okay, let's play ball." He turned to Sarge. "Are you sure you can tell us about the case that's bugging you and play against us at the same time?"

"Does a chicken have lips?"

"Huh?" said Hawkeye, puzzled.

Amy scratched her head. "You're weird, Sarge."

Sergeant Treadwell slammed the ball over the net, catching them off guard. The game was on.

"Hey, you tricked us!" gasped Hawkeye as he strained to return the ball.

Leaning over the table in a defensive position, Amy said, "Good shot, Hawkeye!"

The game was fast and intense. The three players hardly had any time between shots to catch their breaths as the ball bounced back and forth. Beads of sweat formed on Sergeant Treadwell's brow as he struggled to play and tell them about the latest case he couldn't solve at the same time.

"The Five and Dime Coin Shop in Oak Heights—good serve, Amy—was robbed yesterday. Someone saw the car—whoops!—and described it as a light blue pickup." The sergeant paused to catch his breath.

"Did they get the license plate number?" asked Amy quickly.

"No, but I heard the description over the radio," Sarge replied, "and not more than a minute later, I stopped a light blue pickup."

Hawkeye brought his arm back and slammed the ball. It went shooting across, clearing the net by a fraction of an inch.

"So," said Hawkeye, concentrating on the game, "bring them in for questioning."

"Sounds pretty simple to me." Amy picked up the ball and served, screaming, "Kung fu! Chop suey!"

"Uh-oh!" Sergeant Treadwell braced himself and barely returned the shot. "Well, the young couple in the car said they had just come from the bank." The ball flew back to him before he knew it.

"Ohhh!" the sergeant gasped, reaching out with his paddle. "The real problem is that three blocks away—at just the same time—another policeman stopped a light blue pickup driven by another young couple."

"Wham!" exclaimed Amy, smashing the ball.

"Rats!" cried Sergeant Treadwell as the

ball went sailing by. "Anyway, that young couple said *they* had just come from the bank, too."

Amy dried her hand on her jeans. "So you can't figure out who's lying and who's telling the truth?"

"Right." Sergeant Treadwell served. "Or if both couples are telling the truth and neither one should be brought in for questioning."

"Faster than a speeding bullet!" yelled Hawkeye as he returned the ball.

"Oh, darn."

As Sergeant Treadwell trotted after the ball he had missed, Hawkeye called out to him.

"Hey, Sarge, do you have a map of Oak Heights?" asked Hawkeye.

"Here," said Sergeant Treadwell, picking up a map and a slip of paper. "Here's the map and the day's traffic report. The addresses where the cars were stopped are on there, too. Remember that both cars were stopped only a minute or two after the radio report."

"Amy, think you can handle the table and take on Sarge?" said Hawkeye.

Amy rolled her green eyes. "Does a dog have fingers?"

Hawkeye ran a hand through his blond hair. "Wh-what?"

Sergeant Treadwell and Amy continued the game while Hawkeye took out his pad and pencil. He unfolded Sarge's map and studied it.

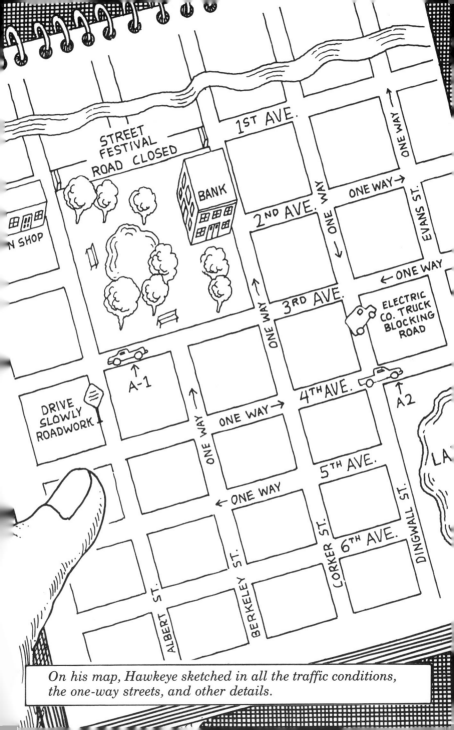

On his map, Hawkeye sketched in all the traffic conditions, the one-way streets, and other details.

Then, his hand working fast, he drew a map of his own. On it he sketched in all the traffic conditions, the one-way streets, and other details.

Minutes later, after going over the map carefully, he solved the case.

"Stop the game, stop the game!" Hawkeye shouted, a smile spreading across his face. "I think you've got a case against one of the drivers. Come over here and I'll show you who was lying."

WHICH DRIVER WAS NOT TELLING THE TRUTH?

See page 79

The Case of the Crashing Frisbee

"Hawkeye," said Amy as they stood in Von Buttermore Park, "just be sure to aim the frisbee away from Mrs. Ratchet's house."

"Yeah," said their friend, Justin, who could never turn down a dare. "Even a quadruple dare wouldn't get me to go back into Ratchet's yard. She's too mean!"

Following their advice, Hawkeye turned his back to Mrs. Ratchet's house, which was right across from the park. Gritting his teeth, he hurled the frisbee as hard as he could.

"Wow!" said Amy and Justin, as the frisbee flew high into the air.

The wind caught the underside of the frisbee and carried it higher into the blue sky. It
seemed as if it might fly forever.

"Oh, no!" moaned Hawkeye.

The frisbee smashed into the highest
branches of one of the huge oak trees in the park,
then tumbled straight to the ground.

"Drats. How about two out of three?" said
Hawkeye, determined to win the contest. "I bet
it would have gone farther than either of you guys
could have thrown it."

"Forget it, Hawkeye," said Amy, sure that
she could throw it the farthest. "We each get one
chance. A deal's a deal."

"Right," Justin agreed. With a devilish
grin, he added, "And soon you'll see who's the
champ!"

"Oh, all right," said Hawkeye. "Okay,
Nosey, go get it!"

Like a bolt of orange lightning, Hawkeye's
golden retriever shot through the park after the
frisbee. In a moment, she returned with the frisbee dangling from her mouth.

Amy took the frisbee from the dog and said,
"Here goes!"

She wound herself up like a top, closed her
eyes in concentration, and then let loose. The frisbee sailed high and far into the sky. But then it,
too, was caught by a gust of wind.

"Uh-oh," said Justin, slapping his
forehead.

Amy gasped, "It's headed for Mrs. Ratchet's house!"

The frisbee tilted gently to the side and made a wide arc toward Mrs. Ratchet's yard. It sailed high over the street, and then began to dive bomb toward the house.

"Oh, no! Not the picture window!" Hawkeye grabbed Nosey by the collar so she wouldn't run after the frisbee.

Amy added, "And not the daisy patch!"

Suddenly the wind came from above and forced the frisbee to the earth. Quite innocently, it landed on Mrs. Ratchet's front yard and rolled to the very edge of the daisy patch.

Hawkeye and Amy turned to Justin, who took a step backward.

"I don't want to send Nosey after it," said Hawkeye. "You know Mrs. Ratchet hates dogs even more than she does kids."

"Listen, you guys," pleaded Justin, "please don't dare me to get it. Please."

But before Hawkeye or Amy could speak, they heard a door open and slam shut.

"Mrs. Ratchet!" exclaimed Hawkeye.

Wearing slippers and a faded black housedress, she stormed out the door, down the front steps, and onto her well-kept green lawn. She went right over to the frisbee at the edge of the daisy patch and snatched it up.

Mrs. Ratchet picked up the frisbee, careful

33

to avoid touching either the daisies or the shiny green plants that bordered the flower patch.

"Well," sighed Amy, "good-bye, frisbee."

But Mrs. Ratchet didn't carry the frisbee back into her house. Instead, she walked directly toward Hawkeye, Amy, and Justin.

"Come on," said Justin, stepping backward, "let's get out of here."

"Don't worry," replied Hawkeye. "She won't leave her yard."

And she didn't. She marched right up to the point where her perfect grass met the curb.

"How many times have I told you kids to keep your things off my property!" she hollered. "I'm about to take my afternoon nap. If this thing so much as goes near my daisies again—" She paused and smiled a tight, mean smile. "—you are going to three times remember that you catch it at Ratchet's!"

Hawkeye, Amy, and Justin remained speechless as Mrs. Ratchet brought back her arm and flung the frisbee right at them. It was a perfect throw—the frisbee flew straight over the street and landed at Nosey's feet. Nosey sniffed it, whimpered, and refused to pick it up.

"That's okay, Nosey," said Amy, bending over. "I'll get it."

Justin shook his head in amazement. "Boy, my mom sure can't throw a frisbee like that. I wonder where Mrs. Ratchet learned how."

Hawkeye watched as Mrs. Ratchet went

back inside her house, slamming the door behind her.

"Probably in a crab apple orchard," he commented.

Amy handed Justin the frisbee, saying, "Maybe Hawkeye was right, Justin. Maybe we should make it two out of three."

"No dice!" Justin grabbed the frisbee from her. "Like you said, a deal's a deal. Just because you two had bad luck," he muttered.

"Okay, Justin," said Hawkeye. He gestured toward the far side of the park. "Just remember, the frisbee's supposed to land in the park—not in *her* yard!"

"Yeah, yeah, I get the message," Justin muttered.

Justin moved away from Hawkeye and Amy. Pretending to be an Olympic athlete, he bent over at the waist, took a couple of deep breaths, and then, uncurling his body, hurled the frisbee away from him. But just before he let go of the disc, he tripped on a rock. The frisbee went shooting off in entirely the wrong direction.

"Oh, no! Not again!" Amy slapped her forehead.

Hawkeye winced. "Way to go, bimbo, it's headed right for Mrs. Ratchet's!"

The frisbee sailed quite gracefully through the air. Seconds later, it came to a soft landing right in the middle of Mrs. Ratchet's daisy patch.

"What luck!" groaned Justin. "It's even

worse than yours, Amy!"

The three friends stood motionless, waiting for Mrs. Ratchet to come zooming out of her house. But she didn't.

"Hey, there she is," said Hawkeye, pointing to the picture window.

Mrs. Ratchet looked at the frisbee, glanced up at them, and gave them a sinister smile. Then she turned and disappeared from the window.

"You don't suppose she really went to take her nap, do you?" asked Amy.

"I don't know," said Justin. "But for a double dare I'd run right over there and get it. After all, I threw it."

Hawkeye scratched his head. "Wait a minute. There's something I don't get." He pulled his sketch pad out of his back pocket. "Amy, will you hold Nosey? I want to go a little closer and get a better look at the yard."

"What's bugging you?" Amy asked.

"Really," said Justin, "it's no big deal. You don't even have to dare me. I'll just go over there and get it."

"Hang on," said Hawkeye, starting toward Mrs. Ratchet's house. "Mrs. Ratchet's acting too weird and something she said didn't make sense."

Hawkeye walked out of the park, across the street, and right up to the edge of Mrs. Ratchet's property. Careful not to put even one toe on her lawn, he stood there, looking at the

"The last thing you want to do, Justin, is go get that frisbee!"

scene before him. He spotted the frisbee in the daisy patch.

"Hmm, something's wrong here," said Hawkeye, frowning. He began to draw the yard. He sketched a line here, a detail there, and soon he had it all figured out.

"Hey, you guys!" said Hawkeye, running back to his friends. "I know what Mrs. Ratchet was talking about. And the last thing you want to do, Justin, is go get that frisbee of yours!"

WHAT DID HAWKEYE SEE IN MRS. RATCHET'S YARD?

See page 81

The Case of Macho's Mistake

Amy picked up the phone in the family room and knew at once that it was the mysterious phone caller. Just like the other two times, the voice was quiet and deep. It was the same time, too: 5:15 on a weekday evening.

"I know you don't like anchovies," said the mysterious voice.

Amy slapped her forehead. "Not again."

"And I know you can't stand broccoli."

"That's right," she responded. "And I also can't stand the pizzas you keep sending. Now, cut it out. Who is this?"

"A friend."

39

"Oh, baloney!" responded Amy.

She knew that when you got strange phone calls you were supposed to hang up right away. And that's what she had done the other two times. She was determined, though, to find out who kept ordering pizzas and having them sent to her house.

She knew, too, that any moment now the doorbell would ring and the delivery boy would be there from the pizza shop.

The voice on the other end laughed. "You want baloney, you'll get baloney. On your next pizza."

The voice laughed again. But then it cracked. For a split second it was no longer deep and rough, but higher, like the voice of a boy.

"Hey, I—" began Amy. She stopped, thought for a moment, then slammed the receiver down. She closed her eyes in thought. She knew that voice—but who did it belong to? And then it came to her.

The next second the doorbell rang. Amy grabbed her bright yellow sweater and raced to the door.

"I got it!" she hollered.

She threw open the door and found the delivery boy with a large, steaming pizza in his hand.

"We don't want it," she said.

"What do you mean you don't want it? You haven't even tasted it yet. It's the best pizza in

Minnesota," said the delivery boy, worried that he was going to be stuck with another dissatisfied customer. "You ordered it, you have to pay for it at least."

Amy pushed past him and hurried outside.

"But that's just it," she said over her shoulder. "I didn't order it. Someone's pulling a trick on me. This is the third time some creep's sent a pizza to my house!"

As Amy ran across the front lawn, her mother came to the door and shouted, "Amy, come back here right now!"

Amy, still thinking about the mysterious caller, raced on. Seconds later, she stood outside Hawkeye's window. Hawkeye was inside, studying at his desk, and Amy knocked once, twice.

Hawkeye jumped up and came over to the screen. "What's up?"

Amy frowned. "The mysterious pizza caller again."

"Well, I've got troubles, too," said Hawkeye, glancing toward his bedroom door. He grinned. "I didn't do all the stuff I was supposed to this week—you know, yard work and junk. I was supposed to rake leaves this afternoon. Mom and Dad told me to stay in here and study until dinner's ready."

"I need your help. I think I know who's been calling," said Amy. "Macho Thornton!"

Hawkeye whistled and then said, "Hey, maybe he's trying to get revenge!"

41

"Yeah, I bet so."

Macho Thornton was always shoving kids around and boasting about how great he was. Everyone always suspected him of stealing things or breaking into buildings. But he'd only been caught once—when Amy caught him stealing her bike bag.

"He got kicked off the baseball team after he stole my bike bag," said Amy. "And he's been trying to get back at me ever since."

Hawkeye hesitated, and then grabbed his sweat shirt from his bed.

"Let's go!" he said, sliding open his screen. "But we've got to hurry or I'm going to be grounded for a month."

Hawkeye climbed out his window and, as they cut across his front yard, Amy told him all about the latest phone call.

"The voice was really deep until it cracked," she said. "And that's when I recognized it. I'm pretty sure it was Macho Thornton, all right."

Macho's family lived a few streets over in a brown, two-story house. There weren't any cars in the driveway, and only the lights in the kitchen and adjoining family room were on.

"Let's go to the side door," said Hawkeye.

They went to the door and knocked. Through the glass, they saw Macho watching TV in the family room. He turned around.

"You can come in, I suppose," he called out.

Hawkeye and Amy looked at one another, shrugged, and stepped into the house. The kitchen and the breakfast bar were immediately to their left. The family room was to the right.

"What are you guys doing here?" he said with a sneer. "What brings the great sleuths to my house?"

Amy clenched her fists and said, "Have you been sending pizzas to my house?"

Macho laughed. "Nope."

Hawkeye pulled out his sketch pad to take notes, and said, "Someone mysterious has been sending her stuff and calling her."

"And I thought I recognized your voice." Amy shifted from one foot to the other. She glanced at the phone, which sat on the breakfast bar. "You didn't just call me, did you? About fifteen minutes ago?"

Macho picked up a TV guide and thumbed through it. "Uh, no. Can't say that I did."

While Amy continued questioning him, Hawkeye stepped to the side. He leaned against the breakfast bar and began to hastily sketch the room for any clues.

"Are you sure?" said Amy.

"Hey, what is this?" said Macho, defensively. "A police station? Of course I'm sure. As a matter of fact, I—I was on the phone, talking to my big sister, Andrea. She's in California working for a bank. She called me right after she got home from work. We just hung up—she wanted to watch the evening news."

Amy looked around. "Isn't anyone else here?"

"No. My dad's still at work and, uh, my mom should be home in a few minutes." Macho stopped.

"Hey, why am I answering your stupid questions?" he sneered. "I didn't do anything. So scram."

Amy shrugged. "Okay. But I'm going to catch whoever's been sending those pizzas."

Hawkeye closed his notebook. "See you later, Macho."

Amy, her breath steaming in the cold air, stormed out of the house and marched down the driveway. Hawkeye had to hurry to keep up with her.

"Hey, cool down," he said. "You don't know that he did it."

"Well, I've got a pretty good idea he did," she said. "Didn't you hear what he said?"

"I guess not," said Hawkeye. He pulled his sketch pad out of his back pocket. "I wasn't really paying attention to you guys while I was drawing."

They came to a street light.

"Here, let me see your sketch," said Amy, stopping. "Maybe we can prove I'm right."

"Let me see your sketch," said Amy. "Maybe we can prove I'm right.

Hawkeye flipped open the pad of paper and turned to the drawing of Macho's house. The two of them bent over it. A second later, Amy snapped her fingers.

"Well, I *was* right. See? Right there," she said. "That *proves* he was lying. And that probably means he is the one who's been sending the pizzas, too."

WHY DID AMY THINK MACHO WASN'T TELLING THE TRUTH?

See page 83

The Mystery of the Star Ship Movie

"Mom, Dad, this is the neatest place I've ever been!" exclaimed Hawkeye as they followed the World Films tour guide onto the set of the movie "Star Ship."

"I can't believe it," said Amy, sitting down in a director's chair. "I just met my very favorite actor, and now I'm going to see the set where they filmed 'Star Ship.' Thanks a trillion times for bringing me, Mr. and Mrs. Collins. I—"

Amy stopped in midsentence as a man carrying a round, metal case burst suddenly onto the set.

"Thief!" cried a voice from outside. "Stop that thief!"

The fleeing man, who was wearing blue overalls, ducked behind a giant model of a distant planet.

Two men ran onto the set. "Guards, stop that thief! He has the only completed copy of the 'Star Ship' movie! Guards, guards!"

Hawkeye slapped his forehead. "Oh, no!" he shouted. "Amy, let's get him."

Amy broke into a run. "You go that way, Hawkeye—I'll try to head him off."

With Hawkeye and Amy chasing after him, the thief raced through the enormous, crowded studio. He knocked down a set of lights, ran past a model of the space ship, and cut toward a corner of the studio. Still clasping the round film canister tightly to his side, the thief disappeared through a door.

"The thief's getting away!" Hawkeye yelled, racing behind a camera and ducking under a tower of lights.

"Come on, hurry!" Amy yelled.

They rushed to the door, tore it open, and found themselves in the middle of another 'Star Ship' set. In one dark corner was the entire control room of the main space ship; in another was an alien fortress.

"He's gone," said Amy, disappointed.

"No, wait," Hawkeye replied. Looking around as he caught his breath, he noticed four repairmen at a work table behind a partition. They were all working intently on a robot, one of the most famous characters in the film.

"Let's ask them if they saw anyone run past," he said quietly.

Just then a white-haired janitor approached them from behind. "Hey, kids, you're not supposed to be in here," he said.

"I know that, but—" Hawkeye pointed behind him. "Someone just stole the only copy of the new 'Star Ship' movie and we chased him in here. Did you see anyone?"

The janitor stroked his chin. "Well, someone did just come in here." He turned to the repairmen. "It was one of those fellows. Only—I don't know which one."

Hawkeye quickly pulled his sketch pad and paper from his back pocket and moved toward the partition. If he worked fast enough, he might be able to identify the thief before he got alarmed and ran off again.

Amy whispered, "I'll sneak around to the other side and see if I can spot anything."

Hawkeye nodded. "Good idea."

He began to sketch the repairmen and what they were doing. He drew in the robot, too, and all the details he could spot.

Hawkeye was just finishing when he noticed something strange. Just then Amy sneaked back to his side.

"I think I know who stole the film," Amy said.

"It was one of those fellows," said the janitor. "Only I don't know which one."

"Yeah, me, too," said Hawkeye. At that moment, three security guards stepped through the door. Hawkeye and Amy hurried over to them with the sketch.

"Look at this drawing," whispered Hawkeye. "We know who stole the 'Star Ship' film!"

WHICH REPAIRMAN WAS THE THIEF?

See page 85

The Secret of the Drug Smuggler

"A drug smuggler!" Hawkeye repeated loudly into the phone. "Wow. Sure, Sarge, we'll be right there!"

He hung up the phone and leaned over the kitchen counter in Amy's house. Both Amy and Lucy were down on the floor, cleaning up the bottle of lemon juice that Lucy had spilled.

"Amy, did you hear?" said Hawkeye, his voice full of excitement. "That was Sergeant Treadwell. He's got a case he can't solve—something about a drug smuggler who's in prison—and he wants us to come to the police station right away."

"Let's go!" said Amy. She turned to Lucy and tossed her the sponge. "You'll have to finish this by yourself."

Lucy sighed, breathing out air through the space where she was missing her two front teeth.

"Okay. It'*th* too bad about the jui*the*," she said. Then she brightened and pointed to a carton of milk on the counter. "At lea*tht* I have that *th*tuff left to write my *th*ecret me*th*age."

"Just try and be a little more careful," said Amy, rolling her green eyes.

She grabbed her red sweat shirt, and they hurried outside, leaving Lucy to finish cleaning up the mess on the kitchen floor.

As they headed for their bikes, Hawkeye said, "Hey, this sounds like a big case."

"Really!" said Amy, hopping on her ten-speed. "And I sure could use a hot fudge sundae."

Sergeant Treadwell's way of thanking Hawkeye and Amy for their help in solving difficult cases was to treat them to huge hot fudge sundaes.

Wasting no time, they rode their bikes down Mill Creek Lane, took a left on Main Street, and arrived at the police station minutes later. They locked their bikes to a Civil War cannon and hurried inside.

Hawkeye swung open Sergeant Treadwell's glass office door and said, "Hey, what's up?"

Sergeant Treadwell's pudgy belly jiggled as he shook a can of whipped cream. He broke into a big grin at the sight of Hawkeye and Amy.

"Come on in," he said. "I'll tell you all about the case while I finish making these sundaes."

"I want a bunch of those little red cherries," said Amy as she pulled up a chair.

A few minutes later, they were all seated around Sergeant Treadwell's desk eating sundaes. Several large photographs were spread out on the desk.

"That's Louie Mole, an international drug smuggler," said Sergeant Treadwell, pointing to the bald man in one photo. "Louie was arrested last year for being the head of a big drug ring. There was a big trial—it was in the paper almost every day."

"So what happened?" asked Amy, her mouth full of cherries and whipped cream.

"Louie was convicted," said Sergeant Treadwell, shaking his head. "He'll be in the slammer for the rest of his life."

"Was that the end of his drug ring?" asked Hawkeye.

"Everyone thought so," said the sergeant. "Louie is brilliant—too bad he's a crook—and everyone assumed that his operation couldn't go on without him."

Amy looked up. "But?"

"But somehow the drug ring is still operating." Sergeant Treadwell pointed to the other picture. "That's Louie in jail. That's his cell. No one knows how, but they think Louie is still running his drug ring."

Hawkeye's eyes opened wide. "From inside the prison?"

Sergeant Treadwell nodded sadly. "And no one knows how."

"Does he ever get out? You know, leave the prison?" asked Amy, frowning. "If he does, maybe that's when he makes plans with the other smugglers."

"But he doesn't get out," said Sergeant Treadwell, pointing to the photograph of the cell. "He never leaves the prison. His mother comes once a week and they talk for fifteen minutes or so. A guard is there the whole time and he's never heard anything suspicious."

"Does anyone else ever come to visit him?" asked Hawkeye, digging his spoon into his sundae.

The sergeant shook his head again. "Nope. Only his mother. And she's the only person he writes to. He sends her a postcard three days after she comes to visit him. The guard reads every postcard. Nothing unusual there, either—at least, nothing that we can see."

Halfway through her sundae, Amy stopped eating. A thought struck her.

"I *wonder*," she said, leaning forward. She licked her fingers. "Can I pick up this picture, Sarge?"

"Of course," he said. "Do you see something?"

Amy picked up the photo of Louie's cell. Something Sarge had just said made her think.

Amy picked up the photo of Louie's cell and examined it carefully. Something Sarge had just said made her think.

"You know, maybe—" she began. Suddenly her sparkling green eyes opened wide. "Of course! Louie *is* running the drug ring—right from his cell. And here's how he's doing it!" she said, pointing to the photograph.

HOW WAS LOUIE RUNNING THE DRUG RING FROM INSIDE THE PRISON?

See page 87

TM

THE CASE OF THE
VANISHING
PRINCE

THE LOOKING GLASS MAZE
PART 3

What Happened in Volumes 5 and 6

Mrs. von Buttermore had taken Hawkeye and Amy to the Florida amusement park, FunWorld. While there, Hawkeye and Amy befriended Umberto, a curly-haired boy their own age.

When Umberto disappeared on the Haunted Kingdom ride, Hawkeye and Amy began to search for him and learned that Umberto was the Crown Prince of Madagala. They also found out that Umberto had been kidnapped by two men who were after the famous and valuable crown jewels of Madagala. With the help of Umberto's two bodyguards, Mario and Geno, Hawkeye and Amy set off to rescue their friend.

They chased the kidnappers through the inside of the Haunted Kingdom ride. But when they came to a fork in the catwalk, they were unsure which way the kidnappers had taken Umberto.

The Looking Glass Maze

"Look!" said Amy, pointing to the control panel on the right-hand side of one of the doors. "Umberto left a clue for us!"

Mario pulled frantically on his moustache. "Where?" he demanded.

"Yeah, where?" said Geno. "I don't see anything."

Amy leaped up the stairs and pointed to one side of the door. "Not all of these are buttons. See? Here's Umberto's ring. It has 'CPU' engraved on it—that stands for 'Crown Prince Umberto.' It can only mean that they went this way."

"Good work, Amy!" said Hawkeye. "One of

the kidnappers was carrying Umberto over his shoulder. Umberto must have stuck his ring up there just before they went through the door."

"Bravo!" said the bodyguards in unison.

They all hurried up to the heavy steel door, put their shoulders against it, and pushed. They pushed again. Suddenly the door swung open, and bright, white light flooded toward them.

Shielding his eyes, Hawkeye took a few hesitant steps forward. "I can't see anything, the light's so bright. Where are we?"

Amy squinted and looked around. "It's not the Haunted Kingdom out there, that's for sure. Look, there are mirrors everywhere. Hey, I know—we just went through the service door to the Looking Glass Maze."

Just then Mario spotted the prince and his kidnappers.

"Prince Umberto!" he shouted, lunging forward.

The bodyguard didn't get more than three feet before he smashed full force into a glass wall. Stunned, he stood perfectly still for a moment, then began to teeter back and forth.

"I—I see lots of little lights," he moaned, then fell to the ground.

"Oh, no!" exclaimed Hawkeye. "Umberto isn't there, he's over *there*," he said, pointing to one side.

"But that's a mirror, too," said Amy. "And

it looks like the maze has the kidnappers mixed up, too."

Amy pointed in the other direction. "Wait, I've got it. Umberto's over there!"

"Prince Umberto!" shouted Geno. "I'm coming! I'll save you!"

"No, wait!" hollered Hawkeye as the second bodyguard ran right into another of the glass walls of the maze. Even the floor shook under the force of the collision.

"Aargh!" he groaned as his body flattened against the glass.

"Not again," said Amy, rolling her eyes.

Geno tottered from side to side, then collapsed to the ground.

"Oh, brother," said Hawkeye, slapping his forehead. "This is ridiculous."

"I'll say. Now we have two unconscious incredible hulks on our hands." Amy turned around. "Look!" she exclaimed.

They spotted the kidnappers carrying Umberto.

"Come on!" said Hawkeye.

With their hands outstretched, they hurried as fast as they dared, bouncing off one glass wall after another.

Amy said, "We're never going to get out—"

Her words were cut off by a desperate plea.

"Hawkeye! Amy!" came Umberto's frightened cry. "Help! I'm over here!"

Hawkeye and Amy spun this way and that. They saw hundreds of images and reflections, but couldn't tell which image was really Umberto.

"Over *where*?" yelled Amy, her fists clenched in frustration.

"Over there!" said Hawkeye, pointing to his left. "No—no, over there," he corrected himself. "Wait, over—"

"Rats, that's a mirror!" muttered Amy. "What about—no, no—what about that way?"

The two sleuths finally found a passage and raced down it.

"We've got to hurry!" said Amy, feeling the walls for an opening. "They're headed out the back way. They'll get away!"

Hawkeye fell forward through an opening. "This way!"

"I hear a car starting!" said Amy.

They hurried around a corner and stumbled down four steps. But they were too late. The car carrying Umberto was already speeding away, spraying rocks and dirt in its wake.

"Quick, the license plate number!" shouted Amy.

The two of them ran after the car.

"Darn!" said Hawkeye, as he strained to keep up with Amy. "It's all covered up with mud."

Amy stopped. "Well, they got away with Umberto. We just weren't fast enough," she said, her voice full of disappointment.

"Let's check for footprints," said Hawkeye. He pulled his sketch pad and pencil from his back pocket. "Maybe we can find something here."

Amy shrugged and kicked at a rock. Suddenly she pointed to something on the ground.

"Look, Hawkeye! The kidnappers dropped something!"

They rushed over to the spot Amy was pointing to.

"It's a map—or just the top corner of one, anyway," said Hawkeye. "It's kind of torn up. Here's the swamp and, and—hey, it's a map of the area. We'd better not touch it—there might be some fingerprints on it."

Amy turned her head, inspecting the area carefully. "I sure don't see any other clues."

"Me, neither," said Hawkeye, wrinkling his forehead.

Amy kneeled to the ground to get a better look at the map. "This sure seems funny," she murmured, inspecting the ragged edges of the map.

Just then, Hawkeye jumped as they heard the crash of breaking glass from inside the Looking Glass Maze.

"What's all that?" said Hawkeye, spinning around.

Brushing broken glass from their clothes, the two guards emerged from the maze. They had simply broken through the last part of it.

"This map tells us exactly where the kidnappers are taking Umberto!" Amy said.

"Where's Prince Umberto?" they demanded in unison.

Still absorbed in the map, Amy didn't get up off her knees. Hawkeye pointed in the direction the car had gone.

"They took off that way in an old car," he said. "We couldn't see the license plate. The only thing we found is this piece of a map—and it sure doesn't tell us much."

Amy stood up and brushed off her hands.

"Oh, yes it does! This map tells us exactly where the kidnappers are taking Umberto!"

WHERE HAD THE KIDNAPPERS TAKEN UMBERTO?

SOLUTION

See page 89

SOLUTIONS

The Secret of the Four-Fingered Forger

"The person who forged the check," said Hawkeye, "had ink on her fingertips. The forger left three fingerprints and a thumbprint on the check. And the only person who could have done that is the woman with the bandage on her finger."

"I get it," said Amy. "The finger with the bandage on it didn't leave a regular print."

The police arrived and brought the woman in for questioning. She later confessed to having forged Mrs. von Buttermore's signature.

"Well, I guess I should have forged a check for only one hundred thousand dollars instead of a million!" said the forger. "But I still would've gotten away with this if it hadn't been for those two kids—the fast one, and the one who draws so well!"

The Case of the Telltale Water

"Now that I think of it," said Lucy slowly, "I guetth I wath in the house. I mutht have left the fauthet on, huh?"

Amy cooled down, glad that her sister had finally told the truth.

"Yeah, you must have," said Amy with relief, "because each of you has a glass of water with fresh ice cubes in it. If you hadn't been inside for hours, the ice would have melted in the hot sunshine."

Amy, Lucy, Buffy, Duffy, and Hawkeye then hurried into the house and mopped up the floor. They were just cleaning up the last of the mess when Amy's father returned.

"Hey, what are you guys doing down there on your hands and knees?" asked Mr. Adams.

"Bernie came in here with mud all over his paws and he got these tracks every-where," said Buffy quickly. "So we're clean-ing it up for you."

Amy and Lucy, who were mopping up the very last of the water from under the breakfast table, looked at one another and winked.

SOLUTION

The Mystery of the Christmas Caper

Hawkeye said, "Leo stole Mrs. von Buttermore's bracelet! Look, there's a message from Mr. Perkins. It says, 'Leo stole it.' "

Hawkeye showed Amy and Sergeant Treadwell a pad of paper on the desk. On the pad was written something that looked like a series of numbers.

"But it's upside down," explained Hawkeye. "When I turned it around, I saw that it was really a message from the zoo director."

"I get it," said Amy. "He must have been standing on the other side of the desk when he wrote it. So from this side it looks like a bunch of numbers. He must have dropped the napkin and holly on purpose so we could follow him."

Mr. Perkins returned a few minutes later, carrying both the bracelet and one very cold monkey. He explained that Leo had snatched the bracelet off of the piano and then had dashed out of the ballroom. Mr. Perkins had chased him down the hall and, finally, out a window that had blown open.

continued

75

The Christmas party continued until late into the night. Mrs. von Buttermore, relieved to have her bracelet back, later said that she couldn't accept the monkey.

"Leo's a wonderful gift, Mr. Perkins," she told the zoo director. "But I'm afraid he and my dog, Priceless, wouldn't get along very well!"

The Case of the Double Alibi

"The car that did not come directly from the bank was the car marked "A-2.""

"Look at where it is on the map," said Hawkeye. "Because of all the one-way streets and blocked roads, it couldn't have come directly from the bank."

Amy studied the map and pointed to the other car.

"And there's no way this other car could have come from the coin shop—at least, not within a couple of minutes."

Sergeant Treadwell mumbled, "Now, why didn't we figure that out?"

He brought in the young couple from the first car. His records showed that they had a police record for robbing a coin shop in another city. When they realized that they faced a long prison sentence if they did not cooperate with the police, the couple confessed and returned the stolen coins.

Sergeant Treadwell let Hawkeye and Amy use the ping-pong table until he presented it to the station at their fiftieth-anniversary party.

SOLUTION

The Case of the Crashing Frisbee

Hawkeye saw a border of poison ivy around the daisy patch.

"Don't forget," she said, 'You'll three times remember that you catch it at Ratchet's!'" explained Hawkeye. "Well, she was talking about poison ivy. See the three leaves? That's it, that's poison ivy! And that's what you'll catch if you go into her patch of daisies!"

"Wow," said Amy. "My friend, Molly, had some in her yard that spread from the park. But they pulled it out!"

Justin shook his head. "But not Mrs. Ratchet."

Determined to get the frisbee, they led Nosey over to the edge of the property and turned her loose. Nosey charged into the daisy patch and scooped up the frisbee. Hawkeye, Amy, and Justin were careful not to touch the dog until she had swum in the creek and washed away the poison ivy.

The three friends agreed to start the frisbee-throwing contest over. Only this time, they decided to hold it on the other side of the park!

81

The Case of Macho's Mistake

Amy didn't think Macho was telling the truth because he couldn't have been talking to his sister.

"She lives in California," said Amy. "It may be five-thirty here, but they're two time zones away from Minnesota. That means it's only three-thirty there. His sister's probably still at work."

"You're right," said Hawkeye. "And the evening news wouldn't be on there now—it's the middle of the afternoon in California."

They returned to Macho's house and confronted him with this. Caught by his own lie, Macho didn't confess, but he didn't deny it, either.

And Amy never received another pizza from the mysterious caller.

READ THE SOLUTIONS IN YOUR MIRROR

The Mystery of the *Star Ship* Movie

The thief was the repairman in the front right-hand corner of the sketch.

"Look," said Hawkeye, pointing to his drawing. "He's using a hammer to put those screws in the robot. He should be using a screwdriver—like the other guy.".

Hawkeye and Amy stepped aside while the guards surrounded the repairman. The man, who turned out to be the thief, panicked. He tried to run away, but the guards caught him and recovered the stolen film.

The studio executives were so thankful for Amy's and Hawkeye's help that they held a special showing of the new movie. All the members of the cast were present—and Amy got to sit beside her favorite movie star the whole time!

The Secret of the Drug Smuggler

"Louie is using secret ink to communi-cate with the other smugglers," said Amy. "And that secret ink is milk!"

"Hey, that's just what Lucy was doing when we left," said Hawkeye, remembering too. "She was playing around with secret inks—lemon juice and milk!"

Amy's guess proved correct. Using milk as an ink, Louie added a few lines on the postcard he wrote to his dear old mother each week. When the milk dried, it was totally invisible. Invisible, that is, until Louie's "mother," who was really his girlfriend, Dora, in disguise, got the postcard and heated it. That made the dried milk turn a light brown.

"And I'll bet Dora was passing along that secret information to the other members of the drug ring," said Hawkeye.

The prison officials stopped letting Louie have milk in his cell and, sure enough, the drug ring folded.

87

The Looking Glass Maze

The kidnappers had taken Prince Umberto to the house on lot number four, as shown on the map.

"Look at the letters and numbers on the top and side of the torn map," said Amy. "It's a coded message. Some of the letters are missing, and so is one of the numbers. The missing letters at the top spell the word 'lot'. The missing number on the side is four. And that's where they've taken Umberto—to the house on lot number four!"

What happens to Prince Umberto? Are Hawkeye and Amy ever able to rescue their young friend? Be sure to read the rest of this four-part series in Volume 8 of the **Can You Solve the Mystery?**™ *series!*